REGINALD F.DWEEBLY
THUNDERS ON !

Malcolm Yorke

with illustrations by
Margaret Chamberlain

DORLING KINDERSLEY

LONDON • NEW YORK • STUTTGART

A DORLING KINDERSLEY BOOK

First published in Great Britain in 1994
by Dorling Kindersley Limited,
9 Henrietta Street, London WC2E 8PS

8 10 9

A CIP catalogue record for this book is
available from the British Library

ISBN 0-7513-7017-7

Colour reproduction by DOT Gradations Ltd.
Printed in China

Mr Reginald F. Dweebly was a teacher. He wasn't very big or very handsome, but he was a nice young man and he loved teaching children.

Unfortunately, the children thought he was the most boring teacher on earth.

As soon as he began to talk, the children couldn't stop yawning, the pet mouse snored, and even the class goldfish sank to the bottom of his bowl and fell asleep.

Mr Reginald F. Dweebly could make even the most interesting things, such as science experiments, dinosaurs, or ghost stories, so tedious that his class began to think about other things and to fidget.

As his voice droned on, they would pass photos of rock stars under the tables and whisper. Some children liked Rick Flick, others preferred Zoot Flash, and some thought Gary Vibes was brilliant.

But they all agreed that the best of the lot was the great Rab Thunder. His music made you twitch your toes, wiggle your hips, and click your fingers just to think about it.

Mr Reginald F. Dweebly never noticed his class passing photos and fan magazines. He never seemed to spot their badges, or the writing on their satchels and pencil cases that said FAB RAB THUNDERS ON. He just went on in his monotonous way with nobody listening to him.

One day the children had to work on their weather project in groups – but nobody could remember what Mr Dweebly had told them to do. Instead they talked some more about the fantabulous Rab Thunder.

"I bet he lives in a great mansion with fifty rooms," said Sarah.

"And drives a Porsche!" said Viv.

"And a Rolls Royce on Sundays!"

Fab Rab

"I bet you he gets that amazing tan in California."

"And he eats in fabulous restaurants, and orders just what he wants, and has loads of helpings if he wants to!"

"Yeah!" everyone agreed.

At the end of the lesson the class elected Sarah and Viv as President and Secretary of the school RAB THUNDER FAN CLUB because they'd got tickets for his concert that very evening.

Before hometime Mr Reginald F. Dweebly's dreary voice spoiled some good poetry and had the children nodding off while he told them about next week's visit to a fire station. At last they were free to go home and watch something interesting on television or read an exciting book.

RAB THUNDER FAN CLUB Sign here

John
Lu

Mr Reginald F. Dweebly cycled home to his dull little house where he sat glumly eating his tinned beans on toast. He wondered why the children didn't seem to enjoy his lessons – after all, he spent so much of his time preparing for them.

But tonight was Friday night and he could think about other things than school.

He washed up his one plate, one cup, one fork, one knife, and one spoon. Then he locked up his front door and pedalled off on his bicycle, a big suitcase strapped on his back. It was nearly dark by the time he came to the local football stadium and thousands of people were streaming through the turnstiles. Mr Reginald F. Dweebly went round the back, chained his bike to a fence, and went in through the Players' Entrance.

PLAYERS' ENTRANCE

By nine o'clock Reginald F. Dweebly was sitting in front of a big mirror with light bulbs all round it. He was wearing just his underwear.

First, he put on a hairy chest wig and a big, gold chain. Next, he put on a purple shirt and skin-tight purple trousers with glittery bits sewn on. He pulled on shoes with platform soles and heels, and a purple jacket with gigantic shoulders and silver flashes all over it.

He still looked like Reginald F. Dweebly from the neck up. But not for long. He rubbed in some brown make-up from a pot marked "California Tan", put on his purple shades, and last of all a wild black wig. When he stood up he seemed huge.

He took one last look at himself
in the mirror.

Then he picked up an electric guitar
and strode out of the door.

The crowd screamed as the announcer yelled into his microphone …

AND NOW FANS, TOP OF THE BILL, THE ONE YOU'VE ALL BEEN WAITING FOR, THE ONE AND ONLY …
THE ELECTRIFYING RAB THUNDER AND THE THUNDERBOLTS!!!

The crowd went crazy!

Rab stamped his foot, the drummer took up the beat, the keyboards and backing guitars joined in louder and louder until Rab began to roar out his famous "Schoolroom Rock".

The crowd went berserk!

RAB!

Next Rab pounded into "Meet me at the Bus-stop". This was when he did a somersault while still playing the guitar. When he played "Lumpy Custard Blues" he split his trousers, and at the end of "Listen When I'm Talkin' to Ya" fireworks started exploding in his wig.

The fans joined in with these and with lots of others they knew by heart.

When Rab came to "Write me a Letter" the crowd hushed. He moved to the front of the stage to be near his adoring fans. There, in the second row, sat Viv and Sarah, mouths open wide, soaking up every sound Rab made. He looked right at them and they just swooned away.

Then Rab strutted into his final song,
"Hometime". With a last crash on his
guitar, a roll of drums, and a whirl of
spotlights, the concert was over.
The crowd went on cheering for
half an hour.

Backstage, Rab Thunder took off his shades, his black wig, and his tan make-up. Then he shed his big shoulders, purple shirt, and sequinned trousers. He took off the chest wig and gold chain and stepped down off his platform shoes. Once again he was Reginald F. Dweebly, sitting in his underwear.

He sat for a long time thinking.

On Monday morning the class came in chatting. Viv and Sarah had already told them all about the concert.

Mr Dweebly took the register and the children prepared to be bored as usual.

But then Mr Dweebly picked up two rulers, did a drum roll on his desk top and some paint jars, grabbed a guitar from behind the blackboard, plugged it in – and whanged out three loud chords!

Then he sang:

NOW LISTEN ALL YOU CHILDREN AND LISTEN REALLY GOOD! WHAT I'M GONNA TELL YOU MUST BE UNDERSTOOD!

The children, the white mouse, and even the goldfish sat up and took notice.

Mr Dweebly sang on:

TODAY WE'RE LEARNING WITH A SWING. INSTEAD OF TALKING, I'M GONNA SING!

"The Romans had no volts at all,
Nothing plugged in a Roman wall.
No microwaves or colour TVs,
No heaters, ovens, or loud CDs."

"If you were Roman what'd you use
To cook your food or hear the News?
What'd you wear or have to drink?
Move to your groups and have a think."

The children couldn't believe their ears,
but they **did** go away and think.

In the afternoon Mr Dweebly began
science by singing:

"When we've planted a little black bean,
What does it need to make it grow?"

The children discussed it
and sang back:

A LOT OF LIGHT WILL MAKE IT GREEN
AND WATER TOO, –THAT'S H-2-O.

And they even enjoyed doing their tables when Mr Dweebly told them to:

"Clap your hands and stamp your feet,
Sing out your answers on the beat
To ten times five and three times two,
It's really easy – try it, do!"

At hometime Mr Dweebly sang:

"We've rocked and rolled together,
But now I hear the bell.
Pack up your things,
Stand by your chairs,
And I'll bid you all farewell."

And as the children filed out of the
door they sang back:

IT'S BEEN A GREAT DAY'S WORK,

IT'S REALLY BEEN
A TREAT,

Outside in the street the children gathered to discuss the astonishing change in Mr Dweebly.

"Wow, that was brilliant!"

"Where did he learn to sing and play a guitar like that?"

"Yeah, … he's nearly as good as Rab Thunder," suggested one of the boys.

"Well, he's good, but he's not THAT good," said Viv loyally.

"ABSOLUTELY NOBODY is THAT good," said Sarah, "because Rab Thunder is the very best and don't you forget it!"

Mr Reginald F. Dweebly,
who was going past on his bike,
overheard them.
And smiled.